EYE SEE IT!
CAN YOU FIND THEM ALL?

By
Sierra Harimann

Illustrated by
Frank Rocco

ISBN-13: 978-0-545-13165-0
ISBN-10: 0-545-13165-0

© 2009 Bolder Media, Inc./Starz Media, LLC. All Rights Reserved.

Wow! Wow! Wubbzy! and all related titles, logos and characters are trademarks of Bolder Media, Inc./Starz Media, LLC.
www.boldermedia.com

Published by Scholastic Inc. SCHOLASTIC and associated logos are trademarks and/or registered trademarks of Scholastic Inc.

12 11 10 9 8 7 6 5 4 3 2 1   9 10 11 12 13 14/0

Printed in Singapore
First printing, June 2009

SCHOLASTIC INC.

New York	Toronto	London	Auckland	Sydney
Mexico City	New Delhi	Hong Kong	Buenos Aires	

It was a sunshiny day in Wuzzleburg.
Wubbzy and Daizy were having fun at the Wubb Club.
"Let's have a parade," Wubbzy said.
"Yay!" Daizy agreed. "A Skippity-Skip
Parade! We can invite the whole town!"

Do you see these things at the Wubb Club?

| flag | scissors | ruler | flower |

Can you find 5 ?

wrench

hard hat

The next stop was Dino Island.
The dinosaurs were playing music.
Wubbzy asked them to perform in
the parade!

Do you see the instruments on
Dino Island?

| drum | ukulele | triangle | maraca |

Can you find 3 🦋 ?

xylophone

dolphin

11

The parade danced through the park.
"Come skippity-skip in our parade!"
Daizy shouted.

Do you see these animals at the park?

| bee | squirrel | rabbit | flutterfly |

Can you find 4 🌰?

bird

dog

13

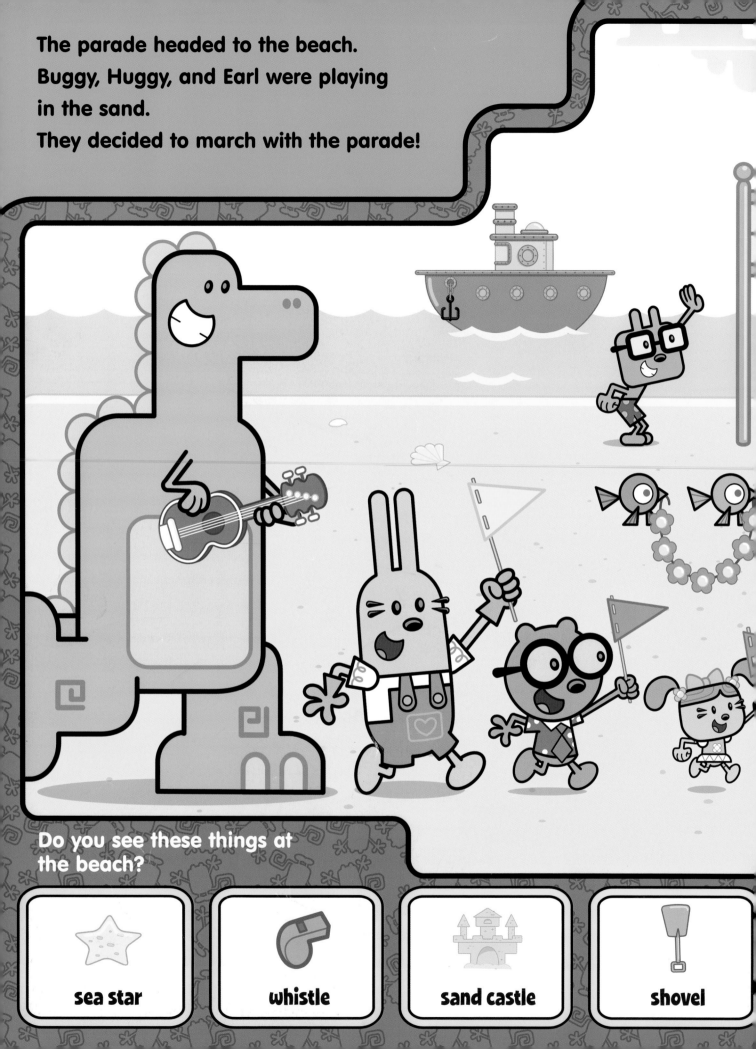

The parade headed to the beach.
Buggy, Huggy, and Earl were playing
in the sand.
They decided to march with the parade!

Do you see these things at
the beach?

sea star

whistle

sand castle

shovel

Can you find 3 🐚 ?

beach ball

whale

15

There was a kickity-kick ball game at the park.
Wubbzy asked the players, "We're having a parade!
Would you like to come along?"
They did!

Do you see these things at the game?

kick ball

apple

baseball cap

juice box

Can you find 5 ?

home plate

baseball bat

17

At the aquarium, the parade stopped to look at the fish.
"Bubble, bubble, gurgle, gurgle?" asked the fish.
"Of course you can march with us!"
answered Wubbzy.

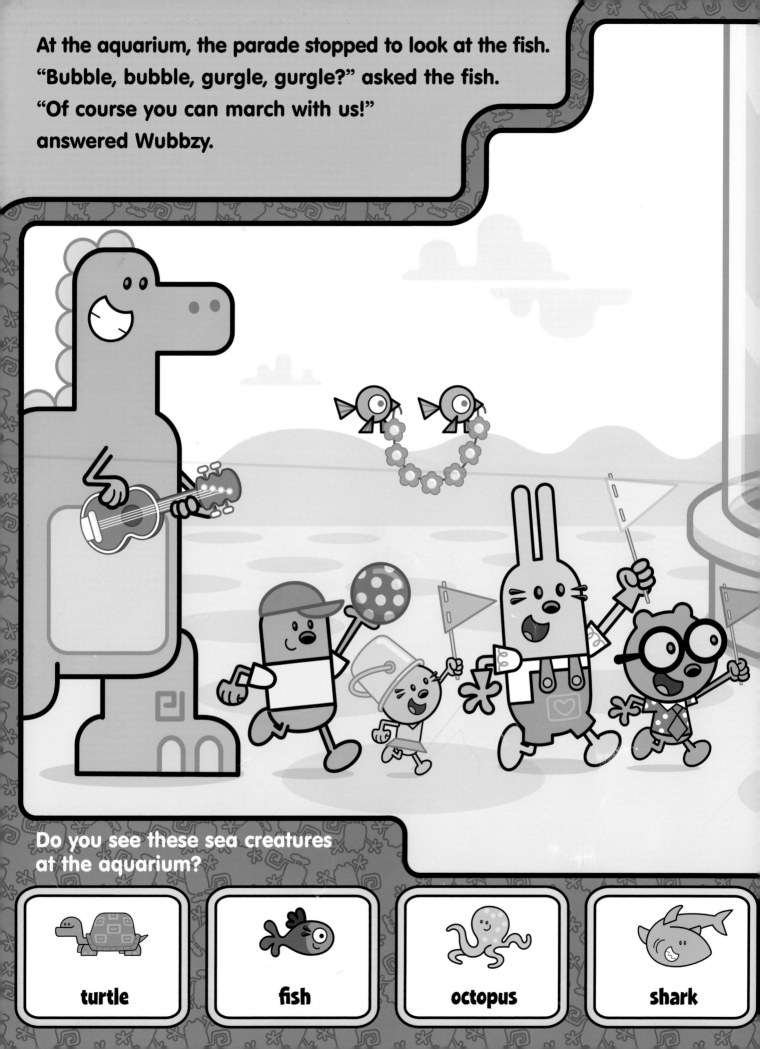

Do you see these sea creatures at the aquarium?

turtle

fish

octopus

shark

Can you find 4 ?

sea horse

stingray

19

Finally, the parade reached Main Street.
"We did it, Daizy!" cried Wubbzy. "It's the first ever
Skippity-Skip Parade in Wuzzleburg!"
The whole crowd cheered,
"Hip! Hip! Hooray!"

Do you see these things on Main Street?

| mailbox | balloon | fishbowl | fire hydrant |

Can you find all 10 parade 🚩 ?

rose

ice cream

21

Answer Key

The bonus items are circled in red.